THE WITCH CASTS A SPELL

BY Suzanne Williams
PICTURES BY Barbara Olsen

Dial Books for Young Readers · New York

THE BOOK'S TEXT SHOULD BE SUNG TO THE TUNE
OF "THE FARMER IN THE DELL." FLIP TO THE
LAST PAGE FOR THE MUSICAL ARRANGEMENT.

PUBLISHED BY DIAL BOOKS FOR YOUNG READERS
A DIVISION OF PENGUIN PUTNAM INC.
345 HUDSON STREET, NEW YORK, NEW YORK 10014
TEXT COPYRIGHT © 2002 BY SUZANNE WILLIAMS
PICTURES COPYRIGHT © 2002 BY BARBARA OLSEN
ALL RIGHTS RESERVED
DESIGNED BY LILY MALCOM
TEXT SET IN COOP CONDENSED
MUSIC COMPOSITION BY CHELSEA MUSIC ENGRAVING
PRINTED IN HONG KONG ON ACID-FREE PAPER
1 3 5 7 9 10 8 6 4 2

LIBRARY OF CONGRESS CATALOGING-IN-PUBLICATION DATA
WILLIAMS, SUZANNE, DATE.
THE WITCH CASTS A SPELL / SUZANNE WILLIAMS ; PICTURES BY BARBARA OLSEN.
P. CM.
ISBN 0-8037-2646-5
1. CHILDREN'S SONGS—UNITED STATES—TEXTS. [1. HALLOWEEN—SONGS
AND MUSIC. 2. SONGS.] I. OLSEN, BARBARA, ILL. II. TITLE.
PZ8.3.W6793 WI 2002
782.42164'0268—DC21 [E] 00-063841

THE ART FOR THIS BOOK WAS PREPARED ON HANDMADE PAPER
USING ACRYLICS, COLLAGE, AND OTHER MIXED MEDIA.

To my siblings, Dave, Becky and Nancy
—S. Williams

To my six grandchildren, Kelly, Anna, Kaitlin,
Michael, Jacob and Justin, with love
—B. Olsen

The witch casts a spell, the witch casts a spell,

Such sights are seen on Halloween, the witch casts a spell.

The scarecrow comes alive, the scarecrow comes alive,

Such sights are seen on Halloween, the scarecrow comes alive.

The goblins lead the way, the goblins lead the way,

Such sights are seen on Halloween, the goblins lead the way.

The mummy lets them in,

The mummy lets them in,

P e a c e

Such sights are seen on Halloween,

The mummy lets them in.

The vampire serves the drinks, the vampire serves the drinks,

Such sights are seen on Halloween, the vampire serves the drinks.

The goblins chase the ghosts, the goblins chase the ghosts,

Such sights are seen on Halloween, the goblins chase the ghosts.

The band begins to play, the band begins to play,

Such sights are seen on Halloween, the band begins to play.

The spooks swoop and swirl, the spooks swoop and swirl,

Such sights are seen on Halloween, the spooks swoop and swirl.

boogie

The clock sends them home,

The clock sends them home,

Such sights are seen on Halloween,

The clock sends them home.

They all change for bed,

They all change for bed,

Such sights are seen on Halloween,

They all change for bed.

The jack-o'-lanterns glow, the jack-o'-lanterns glow,

Such sights are seen on Halloween, the jack-o'-lanterns glow.

THE WITCH CASTS A SPELL

(to the tune of "The Farmer in the Dell")

THE WITCH CASTS A SPELL,_____ THE

WITCH CASTS A SPELL,_____ SUCH

SIGHTS ARE SEEN ON HAL – LO – WEEN, THE

WITCH CASTS A SPELL._____

ADDITIONAL VERSES:

2. THE SCARECROW COMES ALIVE, *ETC.*

3. THE GOBLINS LEAD THE WAY, *ETC.*

4. THE MUMMY LETS THEM IN, *ETC.*

5. THE VAMPIRE SERVES THE DRINKS, *ETC.*

6. THE GOBLINS CHASE THE GHOSTS, *ETC.*

7. THE BAND BEGINS TO PLAY, *ETC.*

8. THE SPOOKS SWOOP AND SWIRL, *ETC.*

9. THE CLOCK SENDS THEM HOME, *ETC.*

10. THEY ALL CHANGE FOR BED, *ETC.*

11. THE JACK-O'-LANTERNS GLOW, *ETC.*